EARTHDANCE

by Joanne Ryder

illustrated by Norman Gorbaty

Henry Holt and Company

New York

Henry Holt and Company, Inc., *Publishers since 1866,* **115 West 18th Street, New York, New York 10011**

Henry Holt is a registered trademark of Henry Holt and Company, Inc. Text copyright © 1996 by Joanne Ryder / Illustrations copyright © 1996 by Norman Gorbaty. All rights reserved. Published in Canada by Fitzhenry & Whiteside Ltd., 195 Allstate Parkway, Markham, Ontario L3R 4T8. Library of Congress Cataloging-in-Publication Data: Ryder, Joanne. Earth dance / by Joanne Ryder; illustrated by Norman Gorbaty. The artist used stencils on illustration board with printing ink. Summary: Readers are asked to picture themselves as the earth, turning in space, facing the light, feeling the green things growing and the oceans shifting. 1. Earth — Juvenile poetry. 2. Children's poetry, American. [1. Earth — Poetry. 2. American poetry.] I. Gorbaty, Norman, ill. II. Title. PS3568. Y399E27 1996 811´.54—dc20 95-6065. ISBN 0-8050-2678-9. First Edition —1996.

Designed by Norman Gorbaty

Printed in the United States of America on acid-free paper. ∞

1 3 5 7 9 10 8 6 4 2

For Lindsey Abdale
and all the
children of the earth
who care for it
and treasure
its creatures

— J. R.

For Joy,
who makes
my world
go round

— N. G.

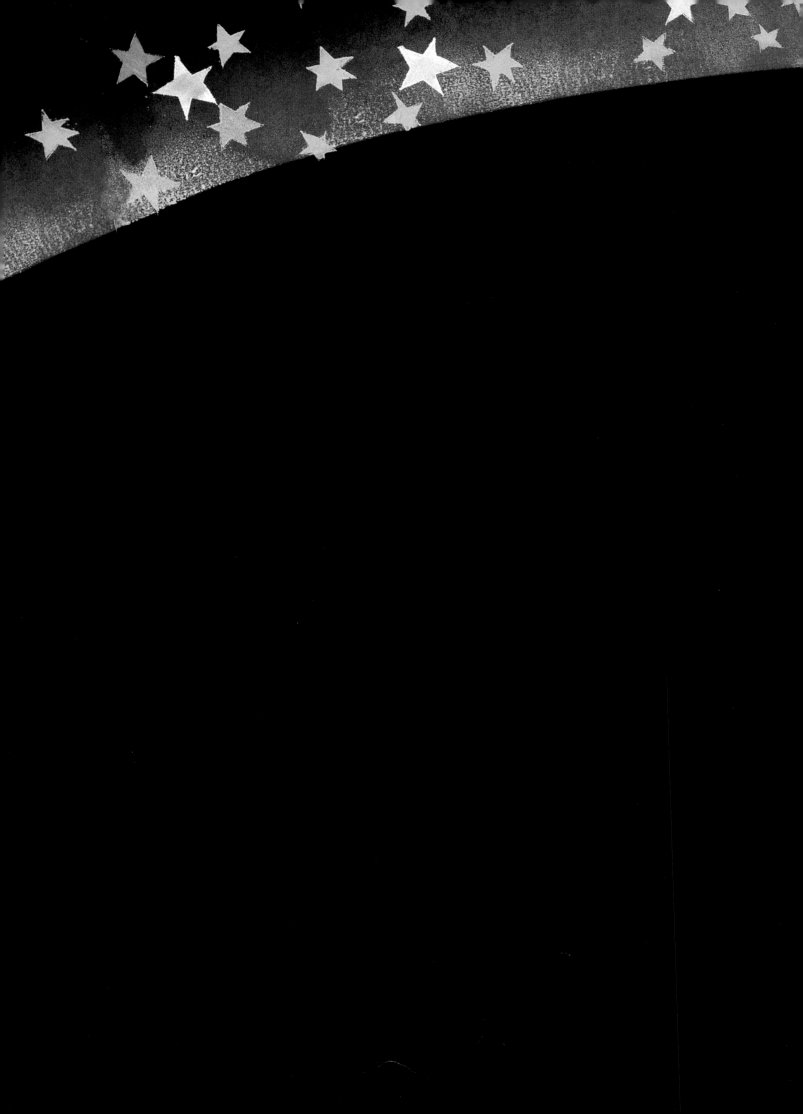

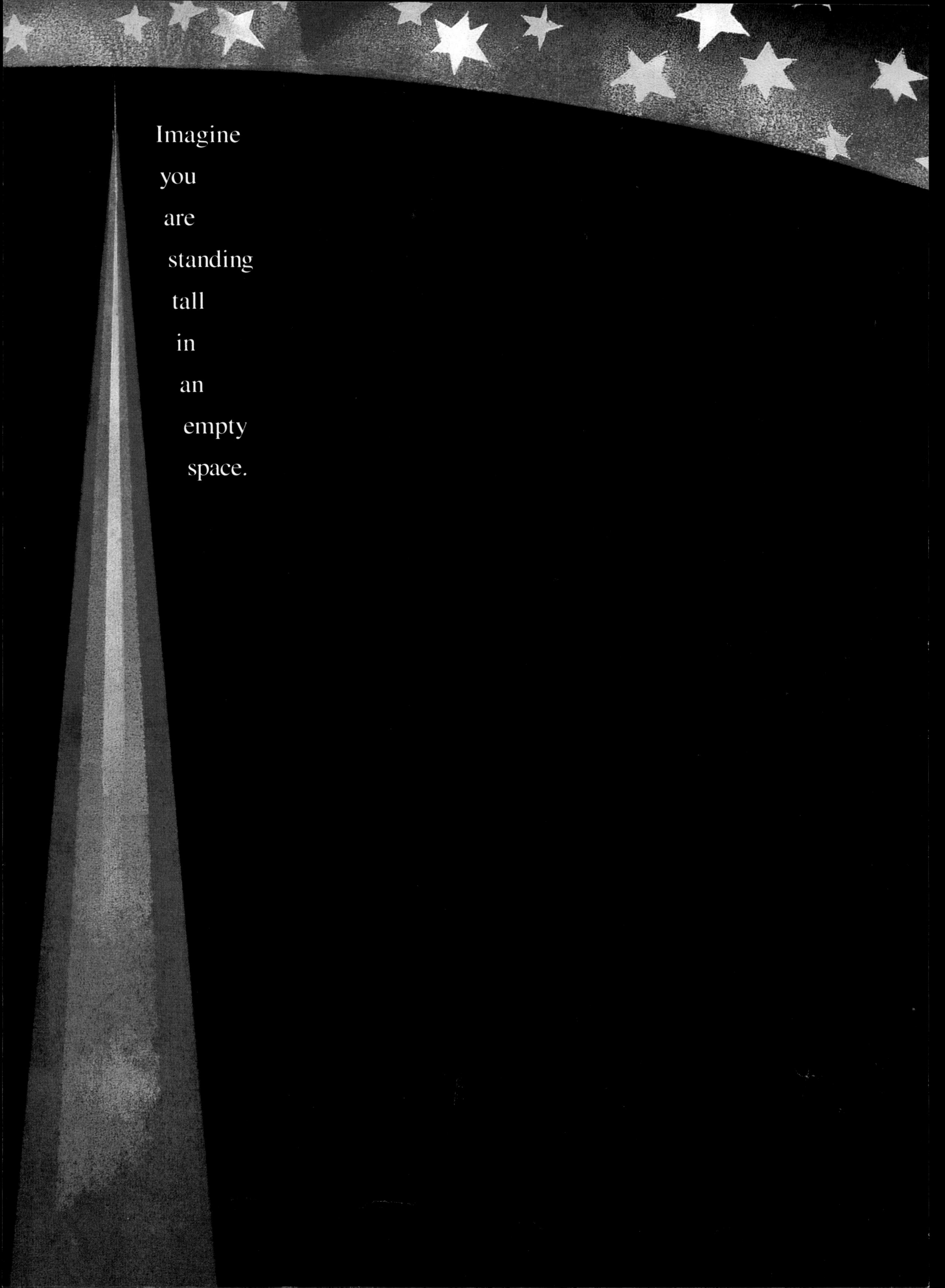

Imagine

you

are

standing

tall

in

an

empty

space.

Stretch your arms out wide

and slowly spin around.

taller than the hills,

Imagine you are growing taller than the trees,

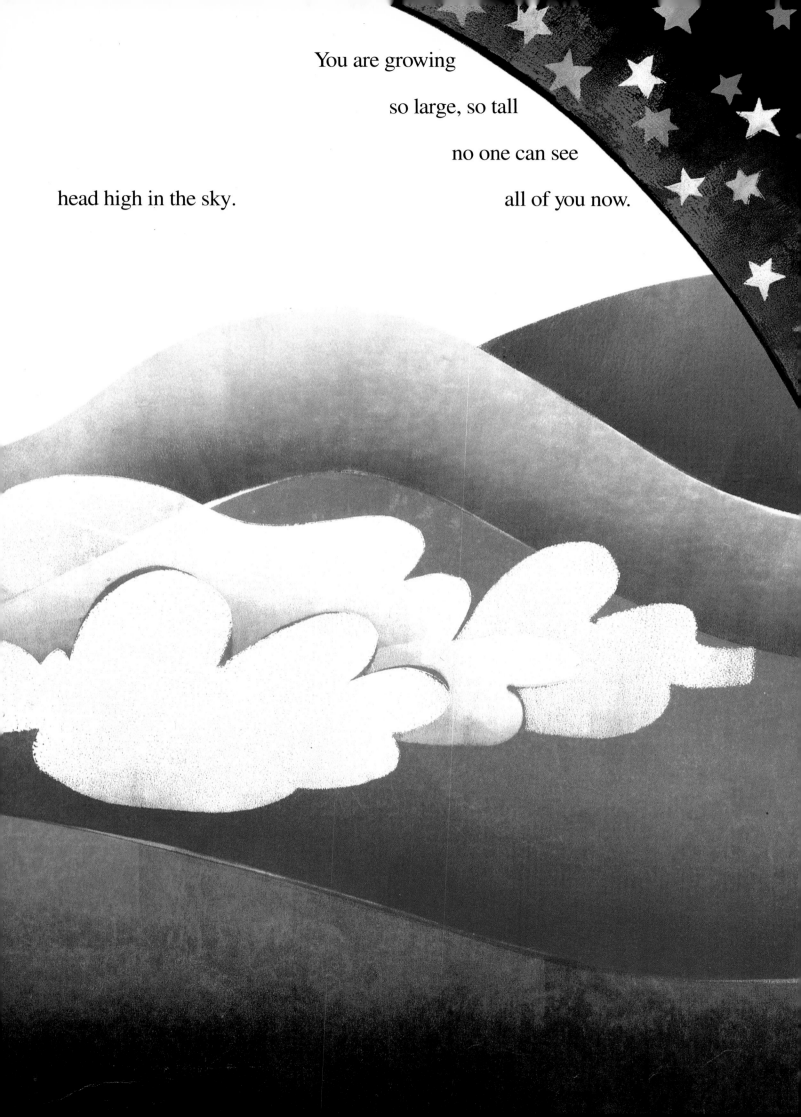

You are growing

so large, so tall

no one can see

head high in the sky.   all of you now.

Imagine you are dancing

space, even larger than the moon.

Spinning around, you are round
wrapped in a quilt of bright colors —

blue flowing seas, dark green woods,
and deserts of golden sand.
You are twirling
so gracefully, carefully,
not even the sand
moves as you spin.

You are large and grand,

and your voice

is the proud roar of

icebergs cracking,

waterfalls tumbling.

Your whisper is a breeze murmuring through the reeds,

a tiny wave

lapping land.

Wiggle your shoulders

and

mountains

tremble

and

quake.

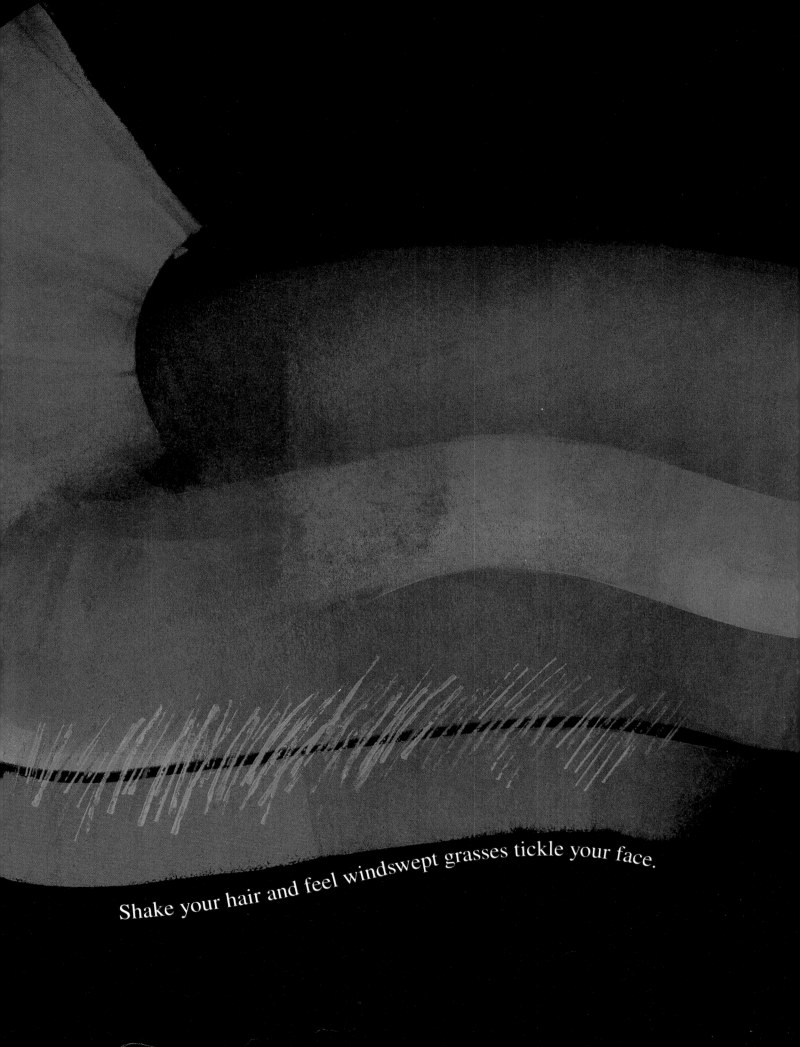

Shake your hair and feel windswept grasses tickle your face.

You are streaked
with roads and bridges,
spotted with farms
and factories.

Up your hills

and down your rivers,

cars and ships

carry people

from one place

to another,

all places on you.

You are where

crickets leap,

rabbits hop,

and children run and run.

Imagine
them
leaping
and
dancing
with
you
as
you
spin.

You are where people meet, talking and singing and laughing alo

Imagine hearing them all, their voices humming as you twirl.

Turn your face
to the bright sun,
and cities wake up,
yawning to morning.

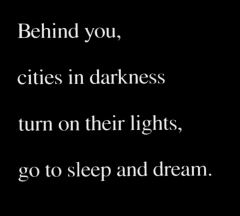

Behind you,

cities in darkness

turn on their lights,

go to sleep and dream.

As you spin,

you bring day

then night

to everyone

who calls you home.

You spin around and also dance around the sun, bringing summer,

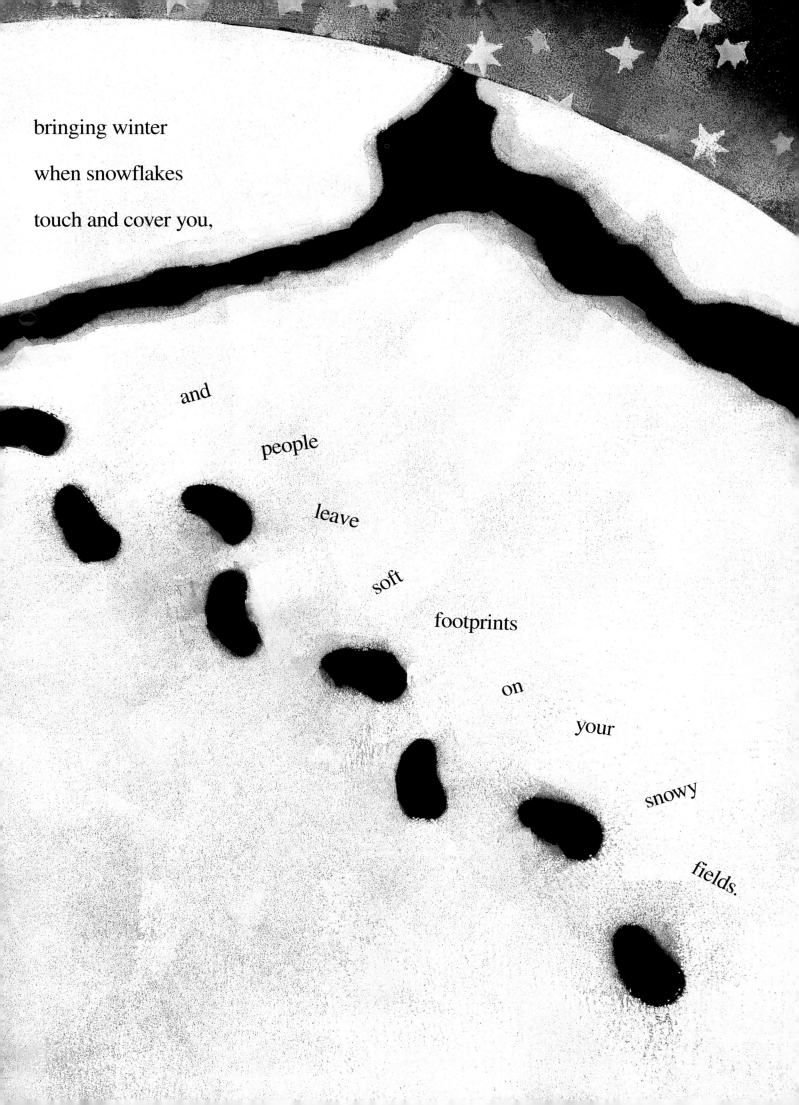

bringing winter

when snowflakes

touch and cover you,

and

people

leave

soft

footprints

on

your

snowy

fields.

You are every place

people rest

and the place

everyone knows best.

You are older

than anyone.

Yet each day

you are where

new life grows,

flowers bud,

and babies

are born.

You are home

    to ants and lizards,

       fish and dragonflies,

        roses and redwoods.

         You are shelter

          for people who

           may never meet

            but share one thing —

          you are their

        home.

Dance slowly,

spin gently,

and carry them

through space.

May they hear

your whispers,

feel your strength

under their feet,

and treasure you.

For

you

are

home.

You

are

precious

Earth